SO YOU WANT TO CATCH
BIGFOOT?

MORGAN JACKSON, PhD

WITH THANKS TO FIELD RESEARCHERS

Jamie Michalak, *writer*

Mark Fearing, *illustrator*

CANDLEWICK PRESS

TABLE OF CONTENTS

PART II
HOW TO FIND AND CATCH BIGFOOT 35

| Bigfoot | Neanderthal | boy | gorilla | man |

Introduction

If you are reading this book, then you are a special individual. You have the courage to believe in the world's most elusive and controversial creature . . .

Bigfoot.

Its name alone can evoke a wide range of reactions — from curiosity and compassion to fear, ridicule, and even obsession.

As a reward for your bravery and open-mindedness, I am about to share with you all of my best-kept secrets to catching one of these hairy giants.

Yes, Bigfoot creatures actually exist. And as I will prove to you, they not only live, they also may be as close as your own backyard.

As a self-taught Bigfoot researcher, or Bigfooter, I have devoted my life to not only finding Bigfoot but catching them. I have seen Bigfoot with my own eyes, and after reading this book, you can, too!

Now, for the first time ever, I will reveal all of my Bigfoot-catching tricks. You don't need special classes or a fancy degree to study Bigfoot. But you do need courage, a high tolerance to offensive odors, and a rock-solid belief in the creature's existence.

You also need a strong belief in yourself. Hunting Bigfoot can be lonely. You might be laughed at and criticized. Just remember: people laughed at the Wright brothers, too. In this book, I will arm you with indisputable facts, so you'll be able to defend your work against even the most narrow-minded of naysayers.

Finally, you will need to be selfless — and release any Bigfoot you catch. No fame or glory is worth exploiting this extraordinary creature.

Do you believe? Do you have Bigfoot fever? So you want to catch Bigfoot?

Then let's go Bigfooting!

PART I
THE SECRET WORLD OF BIGFOOT

To catch our subject, you must first learn everything you can about it. You're about to take an in-depth look at the Bigfoot's appearance, behavior, habitat, and much more. By the time we're done, you'll be a Bigfoot expert, easily able to distinguish the real creature from its many imitators.

WHAT IS A BIGFOOT, ANYWAY?

Before you begin hunting a giant hairy creature in the woods, you might be wondering what this giant hairy creature *is* exactly. Bigfoot's true identity is a mystery, but there is no shortage of theories:

Hoax Theory

If you believe popular opinion, Bigfoot is bogus. It's one big practical joke, nothing more than crazy people running around in wooden feet and gorilla suits. I say . . . hogwash!

Reports of Bigfoot sightings come from people in all age groups, backgrounds, and locations. Could they *all* be making up tall tales? Could *all* of the Bigfoot tracks be fake? One researcher says that it would take about 100,000 hoaxers to explain the many Bigfoot footprints. If even *one* story is true or *one* footprint is real, then Bigfoot is fact.

Defend yourself against those who cry hoax with this list of other recently discovered animals once believed to be nonexistent.

Saola: A relative of wild cattle, the saola was discovered as recently as 1992. Only eleven have been recorded alive, making it one of the world's rarest mammals.

Giant squid: Ancient stories about these monsters were once ridiculed as nonsense. Despite its being one of the largest creatures in the sea, the first image of a living giant squid wasn't captured until 2006.

Coelacanth: Scientists thought the coelacanth had been extinct for sixty million years, until a fisherman caught one in the Indian Ocean in 1938.

Komodo dragon: The Komodo dragon wasn't discovered until 1956.

Duck-billed platypus: When the British Museum received its first duck-billed platypus in 1799, naturalists believed a prankster had attached the bill of a duck to the skin of a mole. It was only when more platypus specimens surfaced that the creature was grudgingly accepted as real.

Okapi: Scientists did not know of this South African animal until 1900. Okapis are difficult to find, given their wariness, acute sense of hearing, and remote habitat. (Sound familiar?)

Alien Theory

Sightings of Bigfoot and UFOs have occurred at the same time and even in the same location. Some believe that Bigfoot are alien creatures dropped off by UFOs, which might explain why they seem capable of vanishing. Are Bigfoot extraterrestrial pets dropped off on Earth for a nightly walk? Or alien criminals banished from their planet?

Giant Ape Theory

Many suggest that Bigfoot is the presumed extinct *Gigantopithecus,* the largest ape that ever lived. It was ten feet tall and weighed up to 1,200 pounds. It's possible that these apes migrated from Asia to North America via the Bering Strait land bridge during the Ice Age (a route also used by the brown bear, moose, and Native Americans).

The giant panda, not discovered until 1869, once coexisted with *Gigantopithecus* for a few million years. If the giant panda overcame the environmental obstacles and survived, who's to say *Gigantopithecus* did not do the same?

Neanderthal Theory

Neanderthals, predecessors of modern man, and Bigfoot certainly share many of the same physical features — hairy body, massive jaw, long arms, broad feet, and sloping forehead. Maybe Neanderthals did not disappear from the earth entirely. Did small groups attempt to ensure their survival by living secretly in the most remote areas of the world? Possibly. However, it must be said that a Neanderthal isn't known for the size of its feet.

Upright Bear Theory

Skeptics argue that those who claim to have spotted a Bigfoot actually saw a bear walking on its hind legs. This theory simply does not fly. Witnesses include experienced hunters and outdoorsmen, some of whom have seen hundreds of bears. All insist that the creatures they saw were *not* bears.

My Theory

Having seen Bigfoot face-to-face, I can confirm that it does not match anything previously discovered. I believe it is a primate unknown to science. While Bigfoot is neither ape nor human, it more closely resembles humans than any other animal on Earth today. For this reason alone, it is imperative that we continue to seek and study this creature that is so like ourselves.

BIGFOOT, HEAD TO BIG TOE

Don't be fooled! To help separate a real Bigfoot from a man in a monkey suit, memorize the diagram below. Knowing a Bigfoot's body inside and out is also essential for studying evidence.

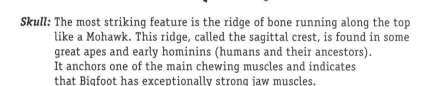

Skull: The most striking feature is the ridge of bone running along the top like a Mohawk. This ridge, called the sagittal crest, is found in some great apes and early hominins (humans and their ancestors). It anchors one of the main chewing muscles and indicates that Bigfoot has exceptionally strong jaw muscles.

Height: 7–12 feet tall (the tallest man in medical history was 8 feet, 11.1 inches tall).

Weight: 650–800 pounds; heavier than two sumo wrestlers put together.

Skeleton: This has yet to be found, but some theorize it is a much larger version of the skeleton of *Australopithecus,* a human ancestor thought to have lived some two million years ago.

Skin: Dark and leathery; visible only on face, hands, and feet.

Coat: Hair (not fur) that is 1–4 inches long; especially thick on the shoulders and head, with long bangs over the forehead. Color can be white, black, or brown, but most reports cite red. Coat color can vary according to the season.

Head: Cone shaped, due to a ridge in the skull [see Skull]; small compared to the body; forehead slopes to the rear.

Face: Witnesses are often taken aback by its strangely human face.

Eyes: Small, black, and round; set close together. When light hits them, they reflect green, a sign that Bigfoot is nocturnal.

Arms: Quite long, extending to the knees.

Hands: Broad and humanlike; hairless, dark, and leathery; thumb is short, but not as opposable as a human's.

Armpits: Glands release a stink gas when threatened (usually unnecessary, given Bigfoot's natural odor).

Nose: Humanlike, with an acute sense of smell; can detect a human scent (unpleasant) from a great distance.

Mouth: Lipless slit with heavy jaws; square, strong teeth are three times larger than a human's.

Ears: Hidden behind long hair, they are small and identical in shape to human ears. Bigfoot can hear as far as a mile away.

Upper body: Squarish shoulders can be up to 4 feet across. Like a human bodybuilder, Bigfoot is strong and lacks a visible neck.

Stomach: Potbelly.

Tail: None.

Legs: Bipedal (walks upright on two legs) — just like you and me; can run and jump over fences easily and climb better than a mountain goat.

Feet: It's not called Bigfoot for nothin': the foot can be 11–22 inches long and 10 inches wide. Most of them have five toes. The big toe is as large as two eggs. Feet are flat.

GROWING UP BIGFOOT

To catch a Bigfoot, you must familiarize yourself with every aspect of its life, including how it grows and develops. What does it enjoy? What is it afraid of? What does it do all night long? Welcome to the hidden world of the Bigfoot family.

Bigfoot Babies

We'll begin with the rarest sight of all — the Bigfoot baby.

Babies average about forty pounds at birth. Like the human baby, the Bigfoot baby nurses from its mother and does little other than eat, sleep, poop, and release earsplitting cries.

The Bigfoot mother is notoriously overprotective. During the baby's first three months, mother and baby retreat into a cave. (Her mate brings her food and water.)

At four months old, the baby can crawl and slowly begins to leave the cave for short durations. The mother carries it piggyback, with the baby clutching her long hair.

After four months, the mother allows the baby to explore. She will frequently place it in a tree nest for a nap [see Home Sweet Home, page 12]. Babies are very playful, sometimes peering around trees to initiate a game of peekaboo. (Resist the urge to play along or risk the wrath of Mama Bigfoot.)

Juvenile Bigfoot

From ages two to six, Bigfoot are quadrupedal (walk on four legs). Their parents encourage them to climb, race, swim, play leapfrog, and uproot trees all night to build strength. At about seven years, they will alternate between a quadrupedal posture and a clumsy bipedal posture, often toppling headfirst as they practice. A juvenile Bigfoot averages five to six feet in height.

Adolescents

Once the male offspring reaches fifteen years old, he is kicked out of the nest to wander on his own, get stronger, and look for a mate. Most of the Bigfoot creatures that people have spotted are these young males.

Mating

A Bigfoot mates for life. Males attempt to attract a partner with a low, cooing call. They show off their physical strength, or display their softer side by offering small gifts, such as leaf wreaths, root bouquets, or raw grasshoppers. (They needn't work so hard. Given the small Bigfoot population, the female, realizing that she has no other options, will quickly accept the male's offer.)

Life Span

Scientists estimate that Bigfoot creatures live anywhere from thirty years to eternity (a lazy explanation for why no one has ever found a Bigfoot's remains). The truth is, without a body or bones, the length of Bigfoot's life is anybody's guess.

HOME SWEET HOME

You can find a Bigfoot in remote, wooded areas that have enough wildlife, vegetation, and water to support it. Most of them live near rivers, creeks, or lakes. Avoiding human contact and noisy environments, they steer clear of cities and towns. (Cars drive them cuckoo!)

Bigfoot creatures dwell in caves and nests, both on the ground and in trees. Some will create elaborately woven homes, while young males are content with matted patches of grass.

Tent nest: The most common type of Bigfoot home, this nest is made by weaving branches and leaves into a sort of lean-to. A Bigfoot lines its nest with moss to make a cozy bed. Nest size varies according to the number of those occupying it. I have seen one as spacious as a two-car garage.

Tree nest: To find this dwelling, look up. If you see a nest far too wide to belong to even the largest bird, kudos! You have found the rarest of Bigfoot dwellings. Tree nests are often used as cribs for Bigfoot babies. (A word to the wise: avoid walking directly under a tree nest. Bigfoot babies do not wear diapers.)

Den: During the winter, a Bigfoot makes its home in caves or mine shafts. For warmth, it covers the ground with sticks and several inches of leaves. Signs of occupancy are pillows, blankets, and Bigfoot-shaped dolls — all woven with strips of bark and packed with grass.

Bed: While a young male Bigfoot is searching for a permanent residence, it will not waste energy creating a nest. Instead, after selecting a safe place, it will stomp on some grass and plop down. To find these Bigfoot beds, look for circular areas of trampled grass hidden behind bushes or trees.

GOOD EATS

The Bigfoot is often unjustly portrayed as a flesh-eating monster. Not true! It's practically vegetarian, relying on plants, roots, twigs, spruce, hemlock, grass, and berries to supply its calories.

Bigfoot creatures especially enjoy nuts and have a weakness for peanut butter — so much so that they will risk venturing into cities and towns to raid garbage cans in search of the salty spread.

Only when vegetation is extremely scarce will a Bigfoot resort to consuming fish and animals, such as deer, elk, rodents, and other critters. A Bigfoot will not eat a human.*

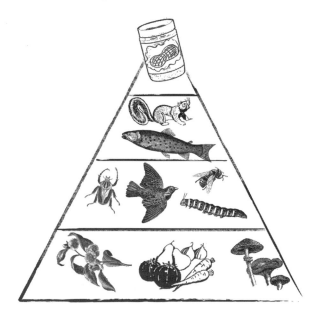

* At least as far as I know. If Bigfoot has eaten a human, nobody lived to report it.

On the Hunt

Bigfoot creatures are skilled at catching fish using only their hands, and they have been seen digging for clams if a harsh winter forces them to migrate to the coast. When hunting animals, they rely on three tried-and-true techniques:

Takeout: In 1967, a man spotted a Bigfoot family digging through a pile of rocks and eating the small animals they found underneath. They dug about thirty holes and lifted boulders weighing roughly 250 pounds.

Shot Put: The Bigfoot puts its rock-throwing skills to use when hunting larger animals. It can lob a boulder several hundred feet and often hits its mark on the first try. (Tip: When tracking Bigfoot, camouflage is a better option than a deer disguise.)

The Grab 'n' Go: If ferociously hungry, a Bigfoot will chase its prey and haul it away to its nest. But Bigfoot won't begin eating until after its stench has rendered the animal unconscious.

15

BEHAVIOR

Despite their ferocious appearance, Bigfoot creatures are sensitive, shy, and gentle. They are violent only when provoked or forced to protect their territory and family. Bigfoot are curious about people but try to avoid them. If they see you, they will usually ignore you and go away. Don't take it personally.

Super Smart

Bigfoot is highly intelligent, which is one reason why it's been able to elude humans for so long. It has a complex system of communication and is quite handy, able to create primitive tools and weave. Some believe that Bigfoot can read minds.

Social Skills

Bigfoot generally travels alone or in groups of two to three. However, on an expedition several years ago, I discovered a group of twelve Bigfoot meeting under a full moon. The group was led by the eldest male, evident by his silver-tipped hair. (Bigfoot hierarchy is based on age, and not displays of aggression.) After a great amount of whooping, clapping, and what could only be described as awkward dancing, they each went their separate ways. Perhaps these larger groups of Bigfoot meet regularly to share information necessary to evade humans.

Bigfoot creatures are fond of sports and displays of strength, sometimes used by the male to attract a mate. When several Bigfoot get together, they wrestle, jump "rope" with long strips of bark, or race to the tops of trees. They play catch and other games using boulders. (Tip: Avoid Bigfoot bowlers.)

Say What?

You'll hear Bigfoot communicating with grunts, howls, yells, shrieks, and whistles. Researchers have deciphered several calls (see Setting Your Trap, page 46), including a belch used to announce a location from a long distance. They also make a knocking sound with their mouths — a sort of Morse code?

Bigfoot are excellent mimickers and can imitate any animal noise, even human speech, to either lure or divert attention.

Sleep

Being nocturnal, a Bigfoot typically rises at 9 p.m. and is in bed by 5 a.m., giving it a healthy sixteen hours of sleep.

Hygiene

Bigfoot is not known for its good hygiene. As a result, its scent is a dizzying combination of skunk, rotten eggs, dirty diapers, wet dog, and the worst human body odor.

Fears

Man is Bigfoot's only predator, but oddly, Bigfoot are not frightened by humans. They are terrified of only two things: guinea pigs and car horns.

BIGFOOT AROUND THE WORLD

Bigfoot's cousins have been reported all over the world, including Malaysia, China, Russia, Australia, and South America. These wild, hairy relatives all appear manlike and walk on two legs, but differ in various ways.

YETI

Like Bigfoot, yeti (meaning "that thing there" in Tibetan) is nocturnal with a stench described as "stinky cheese meets week-old gym socks." Unlike Bigfoot, yetis have snow-white hair. Tibetans have different types of yetis, yet all are elusive, manlike monsters that walk upright.

also known as	the Abominable Snowman
Height	4–16 feet
Weight	300–350 pounds
Physical traits	shaggy, white hair; large, human-like feet; pointed ears; cone-shaped head, hairless chest area
Diet	omnivorous (particularly enjoys dwarf rhododendron bushes and raw yak)
Location	Himalayas

ALMAS

The Almas (meaning "wild man" in Mongolian) more human-looking than Bigfoot or yetis and m closely associated with the Neanderthal. The Alt Mountain people have interacted with Almases f hundreds of years. Not without reason, the local often accuse the Almases of stealing househol items.

also known as	the Mongolian Wild Man
Height	5 feet
Weight	120–150 pounds
Physical traits	muscular bodies covered in reddish hair; human-looking face; massive lower jaw; sloping brow; bony crest
Diet	omnivorous (local plant and animal life); they love grapes, which cause them to sleep for days
Location	Altai Mountains of Central Asia

ORANG-PENDEK

Sumatran folklore tells us that these creatures walk with backward-pointing feet to confuse anyone daring enough to track them. Locals see them often and mention the Orang-Pendek's startlingly humanlike appearance, hence its name, which means "little man."

also known as	Orang Letjo
Height	2.5–5 feet
Weight	unknown
Physical traits	bodies covered with short brown, reddish, or black hair; thick, bushy mane from its head to back; long arms; large stomach; smooth, hairless face; cone-shaped head;
Diet	omnivorous (fruit, corn, potatoes, ginger roots, sugarcane, insects, snakes), likes tobacco
Location	dense jungles of Sumatra

MAPINGUARY

[Sl]ow, but deadly, these large, stinky apelike [cr]eatures have been reported in Brazil for more [th]an two hundred years. Similar to Bigfoot, they [ar]e nocturnal and have a shrill scream. But the [M]apinguary avoids water.

[a]lso known as	Isnashi
[H]eight	7–15 feet
Weight	300–500 pounds
Physical traits	large body covered in black or reddish hair thick enough to withstand bullets and blades; monkeylike face; long claws; second mouth in the middle of its stomach; one to two eyes
Diet	carnivorous (favors cattle and humans)
Location	Amazon rain forests of Brazil and Bolivia

YOWIE

According to the Australian Yowie Research organization, nearly 10,000 sightings of these nocturnal creatures have been reported since the 1700s. Long before then, Aborigines saw Yowies and tell of them in their folklore.

also known as	Jingera
Height	6–10 feet (larger species); 4–5 feet (smaller species)
Weight	500–800 pounds
Physical traits	broad shoulders; slightly hunched back; muscular legs; long arms, large fangs; dark, leathery skin on the face; flat, wide nose; cone-shaped head
Diet	omnivorous (kangaroos, chickens, fruit, roadkill, garbage, lost hikers)
Location	Australia, especially the southeast seaboard in remote mountainous ranges

SAY YES TO YETI

The yeti is considered to be Bigfoot's closest cousin. I myself believed I had successfully captured the creature once in the Himalayas. But sadly, I'd only succeeded in startling a barefooted lama wearing a fur coat.

Thousands have reported seeing yetis. One well-known Sherpa saw a yeti in Nepal. He followed it through the snow for two miles before losing track of it. Other explorers have found some remarkable pieces of evidence. A mountaineer photographed a giant yeti footprint in 1951. It measured a whopping 13 inches long.

Yeti scalps have been discovered in Tibetan monasteries, where they are treated as sacred objects. And a yeti hand kept in a Buddhist monastery in Pangboche, Nepal, was tracked down by a wealthy adventurer in 1958. A year later, a fellow Bigfooter stole pieces of the hand. He took them to India and gave them to actor Jimmy Stewart, who smuggled them out of the country in his wife's luggage.

In 1991, the television program *Unsolved Mysteries* obtained samples of the hand and determined they were "near human." Soon thereafter, the entire hand was stolen from the Pangboche monastery. It has never been found.

Other Bigfoot Around the World

- Chinese Wild Man, China
- Am Fear Liath Mor, Scotland
- Hibagon, Japan
- Kikomba, Africa
- Muhalu, Congo
- Shiru, Latin America

ALL ABOUT ALMAS

In 1420, a Bavarian nobleman being held prisoner by the Mongols, wrote in his journal about "wild people" who were covered with hair and lived like animals.

If the description sounds familiar, it's because Almases closely resemble Neanderthals. Interestingly, as a British anthropologist has pointed out, the region the Almas inhabits has yielded a slew of Neanderthal artifacts.

She also discovered drawings of the Almas in a Tibetan medicine book. The book contains thousands of real animals, and not one imaginary creature. Clearly, Almases exist!

Names for Bigfoot Across North America

• Sasquatch or Skookum, Canada and the U.S.

Omah, Northern California
(Hoopa tribes)

Momo,
the Missouri Monster,
Missouri

• Red-Haired Mountain Man,
Eastern U.S.

Fouke Monster, Arkansas •

• Skunk Ape or Nape,
Southern U.S.

Lake Worth Monster, Texas •

Swamp Goblin, Louisiana

Also: Stonish Giant, Woods Devil,
Windigo, Honey Island Swamp Monster,
No Neck, Hairy Ghost, Ancient Devil

FAMOUS BIGFOOTERS

Most Bigfoot knowledge and theory is based on the studies of a few very dedicated Bigfooters. Familiarizing yourself with their work will bring you one giant hairy step closer to having your own Bigfoot encounter.

Percival Bennett (1954–) has spent more than forty years searching for yetis and Bigfoot, and introduced the use of high-tech gadgetry, including GPS tracking, infrared cameras, and more. But he is certainly best known for creating the first Bigfoot-related smartphone app: "bigfoot finder."

Gerard Lamont (1927–1973) was determined to see Bigfoot get full recognition from mainstream science. He believed in and searched for Bigfoot his entire adult life but, sadly, never had an encounter. He was the inspiration for the main character in the film *Bigfoot Goes Bananas*.

Richard Krupshank (1985–) is best known for discovering Bigfoot's love of peanut butter. This die-hard Sasquatch seeker saw his first creature in 1996 when it emerged from the woods behind his house and carried off his grandmother. (She was returned unharmed.) Since then he has traveled the world in search of this mysterious creature.

Sunshine "Sunny" Brunswick (1971–) is the leading authority on Bigfoot bowling, having witnessed an apparent tournament in the deep woods of the Pacific Northwest in 1995. She remains the only Bigfoot hunter to have seen this particular behavior. She has led two expeditions since then without a repeat sighting.

Hugo Fetipedo (1959–), world-class mountaineer, focuses his research on the yeti of Nepal. He and a Sherpa claim to have summited Mount Everest with one of the white-haired creatures, a beast he described as a "very accomplished climber indeed." Unfortunately, the camera he used to document the feat was dropped into a crevasse on his descent from the mountain.

Morgan Jackson, PhD (1991–) Yours truly is a self-taught Bigfoot researcher who has followed the creature across North America and had more than fifty Bigfoot encounters. My contributions to the field include the groundbreaking discovery of Bigfoot Sign Language. Don't miss my other phenomenal book, *So You Want to Catch Nessie?*

SEEING IS BELIEVING

Eyewitness Accounts

So many Bigfoot sightings have been reported that it would be impossible to list each one here. But your Bigfoot education would be incomplete without reading these classic — and spine-tingling — accounts.

The Welcoming Committee, AD 986: The earliest recorded Bigfoot sighting was by Leif Eriksson and the Norsemen, the first Europeans to visit the Americas. Upon landing in the new world, they wrote about monsters that were "horribly ugly, hairy, swarthy, and with big black eyes." (Considering that the Norsemen were hairy brutes themselves, these monsters must have been very hairy indeed!)

Stinky Thieves in the Night, 1840: A missionary with the Spokane Indians of Washington state recorded their stories about hairy giants: "[The creatures] hunt and do all their work at night. . . . Their track is a foot and a half long. They steal salmon from Indian nets and eat them raw as the bears do. If the people are awake, they always know when they are coming very near by their strong smell that is most intolerable."

Bigfoot . . . Caught!, 1884: In British Columbia, a train crew captured a manlike creature considered to be a young Bigfoot. Named Jacko by his captors, he was 4 feet, 7 inches tall, and weighed 127 pounds. The local newspaper reported, "He resembles a human being with one exception, his entire body, excepting his hands (or paws) and feet are covered with glossy hair. . . . He possesses extraordinary strength, as he will take hold of a stick and break it by wrenching it or twisting it, which no man could break in the same way." Mysteriously, Jacko disappeared shortly thereafter.

Bigfoot's Revenge, 1893: In his book *The Wilderness Hunter,* Theodore Roosevelt shares a story told to him by an old hunter named Baumann. "He must have believed what he said," Roosevelt wrote, "for he could hardly repress a shudder at certain points of the tale." While on a hunting trip deep in the Idaho wilderness, Baumann and his partner found their campsite destroyed. They also saw something curious: footprints left by a beast walking on two legs. That night, Baumann shot at a foul-smelling creature until it fled. In the morning, the frightened trappers decided to depart. Baumann left to collect their traps. When he returned, he found his friend — with a broken neck marked by four fangs. The footprints surrounding his body told the whole story.

Kidnapped!, 1924: A logger was camping in British Columbia when he was picked up and carried off by a male Bigfoot in the middle of the night. The man found himself being carried in his sleeping bag, like a sack of potatoes, to the Bigfoot's den. There, more Bigfoot awaited them. He said, "They were all covered with hair . . . . They looked like a family, an old man, old lady, and two young ones, a boy and a girl." After about a week, the logger was able to slip away. He didn't share his story until 1957; he was afraid people would think he was crazy.

Attack at Ape Canyon, 1924: In the Mount Saint Helens range of Washington state, five gold miners spotted huge apelike creatures. One of the men shot at them, possibly hitting one. That night, the creatures attacked the miners' cabin. For five hours, they threw rocks and pounded on the doors, walls, and roof, but failed to get in. According to *The Oregonian,* multiple reporters and other eyewitnesses saw damage to the cabin and gigantic footprints at the scene. The place is called Ape Canyon.

Uninvited Visitor, 1941: Bigfoot paid a visit in broad daylight to a family's home in Ruby Creek, Canada. A nine-year-old boy ran to tell his mother that a cow had come out of the woods and was heading for their house. The mother was horrified to discover that the "cow" was actually what appeared to be a giant man covered with hair. She gathered her children and escaped. When the father returned home from work, he saw the shed door battered in and enormous humanlike footprints everywhere. The tracks returned every night for a week. The family moved out and never returned.

Bigfoot Goes Hollywood, 1967: In the mountains of Northern California, Roger Patterson and Bob Gimlin recorded the first video of Bigfoot. The few seconds of footage captures a seven-foot-tall female walking across a clearing in Bluff Creek (see The Evidence, page 28).

OFFICIAL ORGANIZATIONS

Bigfoot Field Researchers Organization

In 1995 scientists formed the Bigfoot Field Researchers Organization (BFRO), the oldest and largest group in the world to study Bigfoot. The BFRO keeps track of Bigfoot sightings, studies evidence, and organizes field trips each year to search for them.

Bigfoot Society of America

More recently, this U.S.-based society was established by Morgan Jackson, PhD (me) and several colleagues. Unlike the invitation-only BFRO, membership in the Bigfoot Society of America is open to all.

THE EVIDENCE

It's mind-boggling that most people refuse to believe in Bigfoot despite a bounty of proof, including footprints, video, photographs, casts, and hair samples. Review the evidence for yourself.

Famous Feet

The most common evidence of Bigfoot is the many footprints they leave behind. Footprints are documented with photographs and plaster casts.

> *"Footprints are physical evidence. Someone said, 'They're not physical evidence.' I said, 'How would you feel if I hit you over the head with one of them footprints' plaster casts? Don't you think that would be physical?'"* — René Dahinden, legendary Sasquatch hunter

Willow Creek's Bigfoot, 1958: A bulldozer operator found enormous footprints, 16 inches long and 7 inches wide, near a job site in Willow Creek, California. Newspapers across the country ran the story and a photo of the man holding a plaster cast of the footprint. It was this photo that made the name "Bigfoot" stick.

Cripple Foot, 1969: Tracks of a crippled Bigfoot were found near Bossburg, Washington. Its right foot was affected by clubfoot, a birth defect that can make one appear to walk on the sides of one's feet. It would require an expert on both biology and this deformity to fake such a footprint, making a hoax unlikely. These convincing footprints transformed more than one scientist from a Sasquatch skeptic into Bigfoot believer.

Dermal Ridges, 1982: Footprints found in Walla Walla, Washington include an amazing detail — dermal ridges, the equivalent of fingerprints. These ridges are found only on humans and non-human primates. Even

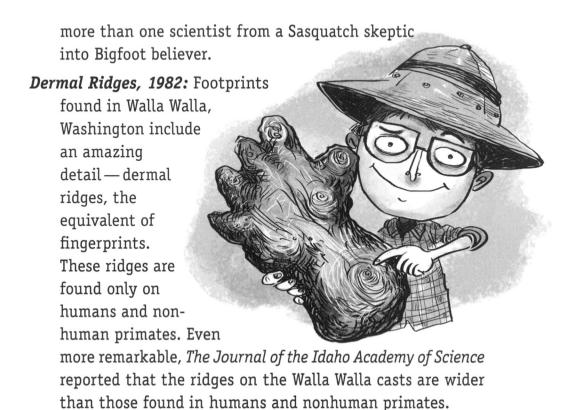

more remarkable, *The Journal of the Idaho Academy of Science* reported that the ridges on the Walla Walla casts are wider than those found in humans and nonhuman primates.

Hear it Here

To find audio recordings of Bigfoot, check out the BFRO website listed in the back of this book. Researchers have captured all kinds of Bigfoot noises, including rustling, grunts, howls, roars, whooping, and long, haunting cries like a woman screaming (a shriek sure to scare the pants off anyone, even a professional such as myself).

One to Watch

The most famous video of Bigfoot is the Patterson-Gimlin footage — a must-see for any aspiring Bigfooter. On October 20, 1967, Roger Patterson and Robert Gimlin filmed fifty-three seconds of a seven-foot-tall female Bigfoot moving across a clearing in Bluff Creek, California. You can clearly see the Bigfoot's muscles rippling underneath its hair, a movement that would not be visible on a human wearing a gorilla suit. Despite great effort and expense by mainstream scientists, the film has never been disproved.

"I can't see any zipper. It looks realistic. I can see the muscle masses move in the appropriate places. . . . If it is a fake, it is an extremely clever fake."
— Don Grieve, reader in biomechanics at London's Royal Free Hospital and University College London Medical School

Get the Picture

We Bigfooters have yet to provide clear photographic evidence of the creature. Trees and shadows tend to obscure its image into a blob. But these photographs make a solid case for Bigfoot's existence:

Mount Rainier Bigfoot, 1995: An anonymous forest game officer was following up on a lead about bear poachers in an area near Mount Rainier, Washington, when he came across this fellow.

Skunk Ape, 2000: The Sarasota Sheriff's Department received this photo of a Skunk Ape, Florida's resident Bigfoot, in the mail. It was accompanied by a letter from an anonymous woman who photographed the subject in her backyard.

Jacobs's Creature, 2007: A Pennsylvania deer hunter captured two images of a young Bigfoot. Skeptics have called it a mangy bear, but even a child can see that the limbs are much longer than those of a bear.

Jacobs's Creature

Mount Rainer Bigfoot

Skunk Ape

Skookum Body Cast

In 2000, the BFRO placed fruit as bait in a muddy puddle near the Skookum Meadows area of Washington state. The researchers returned to find the bait gone and a half-body imprint of a Bigfoot. The 300-pound cast of the imprint shows the Bigfoot's forearm, hip, thigh, heel, ankle, Achilles tendon, and hair. Dermal ridges on the heel are like those found on other Bigfoot samples. A hair from the imprint was tested and determined to be from a primate that has never been identified.

Hair Samples

Bigfoot hair is potentially the most important piece of evidence because DNA can be extracted from it. By testing DNA, scientists can determine what species the hair is from. Often these hairs turn out to belong to deer or bears. But on rare occasions, a hair will prove to be from an unknown primate species.

It is impossible to know if a hair is from a Bigfoot without an actual Bigfoot hair to compare it to. But finding an unknown primate hair in the U.S. or Canada — places thought to have *no* primates living in the wild — should hush some skeptics.

What do you think? Scientists DNA-tested three possible Bigfoot and yeti hair samples. Note the results.

Sample:		Results:
A	Found on a bush in Riggins, Idaho, 1968	DID NOT MATCH ANY SAMPLES FROM A KNOWN ANIMAL SPECIES
B	Found on a Northern California Bigfoot expedition, 1993	UNKNOWN SPECIES RELATED TO THE HUMAN-CHIMPANZEE-GORILLA GROUP
C	Found during a yeti expedition, 2001	DID NOT MATCH THE DNA OF ANY KNOWN ANIMAL

A Word on Hoaxes

Always study purported evidence thoroughly. Bigfoot hoaxes in the forms of Bigfoot photos, videos, and bodies have fooled even the most accomplished scientists. Fake Bigfoot footprints have been made using wooden feet and altered boots. One company even manufactured pairs of giant plastic strap-on feet for everyday tomfoolery.

Where Are Bigfoot's Bones?

If you want to become a Bigfooter, then get used to answering one question again and again: "If Bigfoot are real, then why hasn't anyone found their bones?"

No, we haven't found bones—*yet*. But the lack of Bigfoot remains hardly means that Bigfoot don't exist.

Most animals hide before dying. Their bodies are then quickly eaten by crows, buzzards, wolves, foxes, and other scavengers.

These meat-eating animals devour everything — bones, antlers, even toenails!

It is difficult to find Bigfoot — dead or alive — when they inhabit the most inaccessible parts of the world. The Pacific Northwest alone has thousands of square miles that see little of man. Who knows what might be lurking in those dense forests!

It's also possible that the remains of many Bigfoot were mistaken for the remains of taller-than-average humans. Throughout the 1800s, unusually large remains of Native Americans — more than six-and-a-half-feet tall — were discovered in Ohio, Utah, and Tennessee.

Lastly, I have observed Bigfoot funerals — they bury their dead.

As you'll soon find out, Bigfoot exists. And it's only a matter of time before someone finds the bones to prove it once and for all. Perhaps you will be the one to do so.

PART II

HOW TO FIND AND CATCH BIGFOOT

Now that we've covered the Bigfoot basics, you're probably eager to see one with your own eyes. All your research and fieldwork have led to this moment. It's time to catch one for yourself and show the world that Bigfoot lives.

Without further ado, let's move on to the nitty-gritty—my step-by-step instructions for catching a Bigfoot.

New!!

August 6TH

GETTING STARTED

When
Bigfoot may be found any month of the year, but the peak season for sightings is June–July. Also note that hard winters can drive Bigfoot down from the mountains. Skip hunting seasons.

Where
Bigfoot hotspot: If possible, begin your search in the Pacific Northwest. Two thousand Bigfoot are said to inhabit the forests and mountains of the western United States and Canada. According to the International Bigfoot Society, Oregon, Washington, and California have the highest number of Bigfoot sightings. Skamania County of Washington state is crawling with Bigfoot. The caves in this mountainous area are called "Ape Caves," and new ones are constantly being discovered. Ape Canyon is located here (see Seeing Is Believing, page 24).

Your own backyard: If you can't travel to a Bigfoot hotspot, don't worry. Bigfoot have been seen all across North America. To determine the location of a sighting near you, do some sleuthing. Find articles about possible sightings in your local newspaper. Read up on local Native American legends. Think like a Bigfoot: If you were a huge, hairy monster trying to avoid humans, where would you go?

Scout around: After choosing an area, find a camping site that's near water and offers a clear lookout point. Locate trails to avoid becoming lost. And — VERY IMPORTANT — determine the quickest exit strategy should things go awry.

Perfect Partner

While Bigfoot are generally nonviolent, nature has a way of being unpredictable. Never track Bigfoot in remote areas alone. Employ the Bigfooter Buddy System. When camping, Junior Bigfooters should *always* be accompanied a trusted adult (one who will keep your finds confidential, of course). Leave written details of your Bigfoot-catching mission, including the specific location and date(s), with a trusted friend. Seal them in an envelope labeled "TOP SECRET."

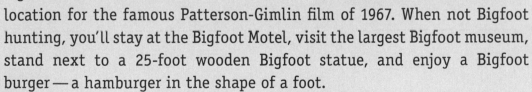

JOIN MORGAN JACKSON'S ANNUAL

BIGFOOT EXPEDITION

IN WILLOW CREEK, CALIFORNIA!

Dubbed "the Capital of Bigfoot Country," Willow Creek boasts more sightings than anywhere else in the world. The Bigfoot legend was born here in 1958, and it's the location for the famous Patterson-Gimlin film of 1967. When not Bigfoot hunting, you'll stay at the Bigfoot Motel, visit the largest Bigfoot museum, stand next to a 25-foot wooden Bigfoot statue, and enjoy a Bigfoot burger — a hamburger in the shape of a foot.

TRACKING BIGFOOT

Like a detective, you must always be on the lookout for clues that indicate a Bigfoot is near. Search for huge footprints, clumps of long hair, and possible Bigfoot nests. Using brightly colored flags, mark the places where you find evidence. These are good spots to build your trap.

Footprints

The most obvious sign of Bigfoot is, well, its enormous footprint! It should be twice as long as yours and up to three times as wide (see page 9). A Bigfoot footprint is typically 11 to 22 inches long and as much as 10 inches wide. The footprint should be flat (with no arch) and about 3½ inches deep, showing that it was made by something heavy.

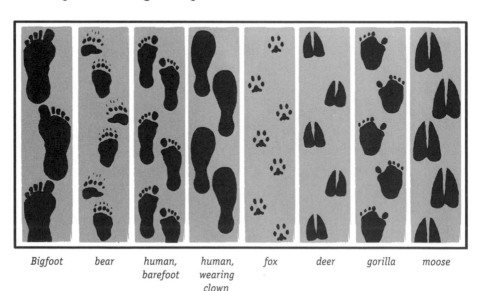

| Bigfoot | bear | human, barefoot | human, wearing clown shoes | fox | deer | gorilla | moose |

Tracks: If you see more than one footprint, measure the space in between them. A Bigfoot takes steps that are twice the length of an average man's, so the steps should be at least six feet apart. They should also be tightly aligned in single file, narrower than a human trail.

"When you have eliminated the impossible, whatever remains, however improbable, must be the truth."

— Sherlock Holmes (Sir Arthur Conan Doyle)

Nests

Bigfoot creatures dwell in trees, caves, and on the ground (see page 12). To find a Bigfoot home, scan the base of every tree. Do you see one with several branches propped up against it to form a lean-to? Chances are you've just found yourself a Bigfoot nest!

If you don't spot one right away, don't be discouraged. Many clues can lead you to a nest: Do you see any broken tree limbs snapped or twisted about eight feet up? (This type of twisting can be made only by a creature with enormous strength and a powerful grip.) Are there many Bigfoot footprints in one area? Do the animals around you seem bug-eyed and skittish? If you've answered yes to any one of these questions, a nest should be nearby.

Once you find a nest, check the bed inside to see if it's still being used. If the bed has a body indention, your Bigfoot is within one to three miles of you.

Photograph and videotape the nest as evidence.

Poop

Scat, or poop, is an important way of identifying different types of animals, as well as their diets. What distinguishes Bigfoot scat from that of any other is its enormous size. A typical specimen is between two to three feet long.

Use the chart below to determine if the droppings you find are Bigfoot scat. If so, collect it as evidence.

BE SAFE. Scat is germy. Always wear latex gloves and use tongs or tweezers to pick up your sample. Avoid inhaling. Place the poop in a plastic bag, label it, and immediately place the bag in a cooler. Do NOT use the same cooler you're using to store food. Once home, store your bag(s) in the freezer until ready to take to a lab.

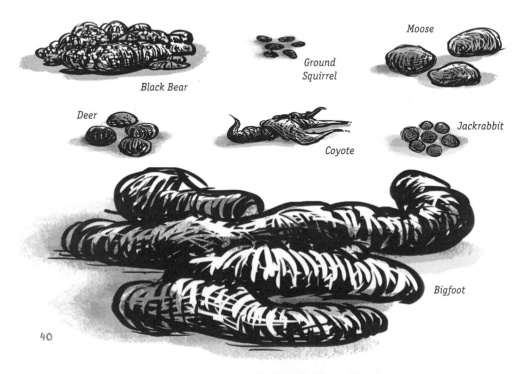

Black Bear

Ground Squirrel

Moose

Deer

Coyote

Jackrabbit

Bigfoot

Things to note:

1. Where did you find the scat?
2. What time of day did you find it?
3. How old do you think the droppings are?
4. Determine the size in both length and width.
5. Is there one dropping or are there multiple ones?
6. Can you identify any hair or undigested food particles?
7. Note the color, which is a result of the animal's diet.
8. What is the consistency? (Typically, the softer the scat, the fresher it is — a clue to tell you if Bigfoot is close!)

Where is all the Bigfoot poop? It is extremely rare to find Bigfoot droppings. I have observed several Bigfoot practices that account for its apparent absence. They often use their nests as latrines (hence the creature's vile odor). If Bigfoot *must* use an area outside the nest, they politely bury their business. And if they do not, the scat is quickly taken care of by nature anyway.

Hair

Carefully examine all footprints, trees, bushes, and fences for long strands of hair, often found in clumps. Using tweezers, collect all the hair samples you find. Place each sample in a plastic bag. Label the bag with the date, time, and location for later DNA testing.

Other Signs of Bigfoot

Unusual noises: Before you go out seeking Bigfoot, it's a good idea to learn the noises of coyotes, wolves, dogs, bears, birds, and other animals in the area. This knowledge will make it easier for you to distinguish a Bigfoot's call. That said, be aware that Bigfoot are masters of mimicking other animals to lure in prey or mislead humans. They are famous for their spot-on owl hoots. Use a tape recorder to capture possible Bigfoot sounds.

Howling dogs: Dogs react loudly and swiftly to Bigfoot's presence. If dogs appear spooked, a Bigfoot could be extremely close.

Horrible odor: Follow your nose. There is no mistaking a Bigfoot's stench.

Warnings: Earth-shattering screams, log barricades, flying boulders . . . A Bigfoot has many tactics for dissuading humans from entering its territory. These warnings may seem terrifying, but stay put. If you appear nonthreatening, you probably won't be harmed.

THE STAKEOUT

Pack Your Bags

Poor preparation could lead to a hair-raising situation. Plan to spend several nights at your chosen location and gather the necessary supplies and Bigfoot-catching equipment. Triple-check to make sure you didn't forget anything.

What NOT to pack: Bigfoot have a keen sense of smell. Avoid packing perfume, deodorant, breath mints, and other pleasantly scented items that might alert a Bigfoot to your presence and keep it away.

Tips for photographing Bigfoot: Wear the camera around your neck at all times. If you see Bigfoot, take as many photos as you can *immediately*. If you wait for it to come closer before taking pictures, it will likely retreat. The last thing the world needs is another blurry photo of Bigfoot hiding in the shadows.

Things You'll Need:

- ○ Camouflage netting
- ○ Night-vision goggles
- ○ Tent
- ○ Sleeping bag
- ○ Binoculars
- ○ Emergency sirens
- ○ Whistles
- ○ Nose clip (A Bigfoot's smell has caused some to pass out.)
- ○ Camcorder with night vision
- ○ TWO cameras with night vision (an extra for backup)
- ○ Tape recorders
- ○ Tape of vocalizations (optional)
- ○ Supplies for building a trap
- ○ Supplies for gathering evidence: latex gloves, tongs, tweezers, plastic bags, marker for labeling specimens
- ○ TWO coolers — one for food and one for scat (Careful not to mix these up!)
- ○ Journal for recording data
- ○ Equipment for making casts of footprints
- ○ Tranquilizer gun
- ○ Flashlight
- ○ Protective metallic suit
- ○ Disguise and/or camouflage gear
- ○ Meals, eating utensils, a thermos, and lots of coffee or hot chocolate
- ○ *So You Want to Catch Bigfoot?* (this book!)

SETTING YOUR TRAP

For the first time ever, I'm providing step-by-step instructions to constructing, baiting, and using three of my most foolproof Bigfoot traps!

After choosing the trap that is best for you, build and set it during the day while Bigfoot are asleep. Then wait until nightfall to catch one.

The Peanut-Butter Trap

Bigfoot are nuts about peanut butter, making this a trap they can't resist. How it works in a nutshell: A net is hung from a tree. Peanut-butter jars are attached to the net. When a Bigfoot yanks on a jar, the net falls on it, and — wham! — you've snagged your first Sasquatch.

What you'll need:

30 jars of peanut butter	glue
30 pieces of string (3 feet each)	leaves
net or hammock	twigs
old hooded sweatshirt (large)	berries (any kind will do)
old baseball cap	

1. Create a berry-bush disguise. Glue leaves, twigs, and berries onto the sweatshirt and cap. Set aside.

2. Hang a large net from various branches of a tree. Make sure the netting is hidden among the leaves and not in sight.

3. Tie thirty peanut-butter jars to the netting. They should dangle low enough for Bigfoot to see and reach.

4. Put on your disguise.

5. Hide and wait.

Letting Bigfoot Go
Untie several jars of peanut butter from the net and quickly roll them over to the Bigfoot. While it's distracted by the peanut butter, slowly begin pulling the net off and throw more jars as far as you can into the woods. The Bigfoot will chase the jars, not you.

The Holey Moley Trap

If you are a strong person with lots of free time — or happen to have access to an excavator — then this is the trap for you. An oldie but goodie.

What you'll need:

large shovel or excavator	leaves and branches
wheelbarrow	pillow
large net	blanket
fruit (apples work well)	Bigfoot snacks — leaves, berries, roots, insects
string (2 feet)	rope (30 feet)

1. At the base of a tree, dig a 20' x 9' hole. It should be big enough to keep the Bigfoot from escaping once inside.

2. Using a wheelbarrow, take the dirt you've dug up and place it far away from the hole. Bigfoot are not dumb, and the sudden appearance of a dirt mountain is sure to make them suspicious.

3. Make the hole comfortable for a Bigfoot by furnishing it with a blanket, pillow, and some tasty snacks.

4. Cover the hole with a net.

5. Completely cover the net with a thick layer of leaves and small branches.

6. Bait the Bigfoot trap by hanging some fruit on a branch about 8–10 feet above the hole.

7. Climb the tree, hide, and wait. (I explain where the rope comes in below.)

Letting Bigfoot Go
Tie one end of the rope around the base of a tree at least ten feet away from the hole. Grabbing the long end of the rope, climb the tree. When you're at a safe height, throw the rope into the hole. The Bigfoot will use it to climb free. With luck, he won't look up.

The Classic Box Trap

This simple trap was inspired by the world's only permanent Bigfoot trap, located in the Siskiyou National Forest of Oregon. The Siskiyou trap has never actually caught a Bigfoot, but perhaps you will have better luck.

What you'll need:

    10' x 10' x 10' wooden box (a size roomy enough for your catch)
    large stick
    2 ropes (20 feet each)
    metal eye large enough for the rope to go through
    leaves, branches, dirt
    5 peanut-butter sandwiches
    camouflage or disguise (See Step 1 of the Peanut-Butter Trap)

1. Cut a 3' x 3' window into the box.

2. Screw the metal eye into the top center of the box.

3. Fasten a rope to the eye. (You'll use this rope to free the Bigfoot later.)

4. Prop up the box with the stick.

5. Tie one end of the second rope to the stick.

6. Cover the box with leaves, branches, and dirt.

7. Place the peanut-butter sandwiches under the box.

8. Put on your camouflage or disguise.

9. Holding an end of the second rope, hide behind a tree and wait.

10. When the Bigfoot reaches for a sandwich, pull the rope to trap the creature under the box.

Letting Bigfoot Go
You must follow two steps: (1) Pull the rope that's attached to the top of the box; and (2) *run.*

Here, Bigfoot, Bigfoot, Bigfoot!

The trap is set. You are finally ready to attract your Bigfoot. Remember: *You don't go to Bigfoot. Bigfoot comes to you.*

You might have heard that it is best to remain silent while trying to lure your catch, but I disagree. I've had tremendous success in calling Bigfoot.

It is crucial that you practice and perfect the calls *before* trying them on any Bigfoot. Call the wrong thing, and the one caught could be you!

How to Ape Bigfoot:

Whooooo
Woo-OOP, woo-OOP, woo-OOP........This common call is used as a sort of dinner bell.

Whistle.............................A six-second whistle says, "Do you want to play?" This call attracts juvenile Bigfoot interested in a game, like knock-down-a-tree. (Do NOT use this call if you are sitting in a tree.)

Belch..............................Bigfoot release loud belching vocalizations to let others know where they are located. For practice tips, ask the nearest 6–12-year-old boy.

Aye-yi-YI!.......................A distressed Bigfoot will let out a piercing, high-pitched, bloodcurdling shriek that sounds like a woman screaming. Use this as a last resort. Bigfoot do not take kindly to those who cry human.

Coo, coo.........................The Bigfoot's mating call is a low cooing sound. Another call to use sparingly. If things go wrong, you could end up a Bigfoot bride.

The Waiting (is the hardest part)

Most likely, you will not see a Bigfoot on your first night. But if you feel like you're being watched, you probably are. It could take several days before these shy creatures become used to your presence and resume their normal activities. As a result, an enormous portion of a Bigfoot expedition is spent waiting.

So get comfortable. Be still. Tune in to your surroundings. The density of woods, light, and shadow make it difficult to spot a Bigfoot right away. Look carefully at the trees. Is one of those trunks actually a Bigfoot?

CAUGHT!

Huzzah! You did it! You've caught your first Bigfoot!

CONGRATULATIONS!

How do you feel? Nervous? Excited? Scared? All of the above?

Well, take a deep breath. Do not let your Bigfoot see you until you are calm. Never show fear. Your body language should be relaxed and in control. You want the Bigfoot to feel completely at ease with you.

Wait until daylight to approach it. The Bigfoot will be safe in the trap until morning. When ready, step toward it with your left hand over your heart to show that you mean no harm.

The Bigfoot might stare at you without emotion or expression. This is a common reaction. Don't let it keep you from trying the next step — communicating with your Bigfoot.

Bigfoot Sign Language

I have discovered that humans can communicate with Bigfoot using Bigfoot Sign Language. Below are a few key phrases.

I am your friend.

a disgusting smell or human

I will not eat/hurt you.

car

Run for your life! or GUINEA PIG!

Yes

Don't come any closer.

I am thirsty.

No

I am hungry.

Experiment by trying other signs of your creation. In your journal, record all of the Bigfoot's responses, including those you don't understand. You can attempt to decipher them later.

Gathering Proof

Begin to collect evidence, staying a safe distance from the trap. Do not get so wrapped up in your work that you place yourself in a hairy situation.

- *Photograph your Bigfoot. Capture its full body, as well as close-ups of its face, hands, and feet.*

- *Videotape your find while testing its intelligence. Offer it various objects after demonstrating how they work. What does it do with a mirror? A hairbrush? A pogo stick? Bubble gum?*

- *Photograph and make casts of both individual footprints and the entire track.*

- *Collect scat. (Remember to use your nose clip!)*

- *Collect any hair shed outside the trap.*

- *Do NOT get inside the trap.*

Catch and Release

You have caught your Bigfoot. Now what? Do you show your Bigfoot to the world and gain fame and glory? Or do you set it free?

It's a question that Bigfooters don't entirely agree upon. Some argue that the only way to protect the creature is to prove that it exists, and the only way to do that is to capture and kill one. Others strongly disagree.

I am confident that you will not harm a Bigfoot. I would not have written this book if I believed you would. Because once you meet one, you will understand why not a single Bigfoot has been killed or held captive. Look one in the eyes. They're like us.

Say Good-Bye

You might find it difficult to part ways with your Bigfoot. You may have shared some good times and grown attached. If you worry that you'll never see each other again, let me reassure you that if you have been kind, you will. These creatures have a nearly photographic memory. If you've gained the Bigfoot's trust, then the next time you appear in its territory, it will approach you—no traps necessary.

Clean Up

Leave the woods exactly as you found them. Pack up all your belongings and trash. Collect any evidence left inside the trap. Remove all traps and fill the hole back in, so no poor animals will be caught while you're gone.

Report the Evidence

After testing your evidence, report it to the Bigfoot Field Researchers Organization (BFRO). If you've followed all my directions, then the proof you've found will make history!

A Job Well Done

And here, fellow Bigfooter, is where I leave you. You've come a long way from the first pages of this book, and for that, I applaud you. Bravo!

Now that you've seen your first Bigfoot, you'll probably want to see them again and again. I urge you to do so. Now, more than ever, the Bigfoot community needs energetic souls dedicated to furthering Bigfoot research. Our field is still relatively new; there is much left to learn about this mysterious creature. It is our duty to both study and protect them. As Bigfoot advocates, we must work to conserve the pristine forests and mountains that these creatures call home.

Still, it is inevitable that one day—perhaps sooner than we think—Bigfoot will be forced out of the shadows and into the light. When this day comes, mainstream science will finally have to accept Bigfoot.

I must admit, I sometimes hope that Bigfoot remains elusive to non-believers. It would be a great tragedy if a Bigfoot were exploited or harmed in any way. I will continue to let every Bigfoot I catch go and keep its exact whereabouts a secret. Will you do the same?

Good luck, and happy Bigfooting!

GLOSSARY

anthropology: the science of human beings and their ancestors

Australopithecus: an extinct human ancestor thought to have lived some two million years ago

Bigfooter: a general term used to describe a Bigfoot enthusiast. Bigfooters range from armchair amateurs to expert researchers and hunters.

biped: an animal or person that walks on two feet

carnivore: a flesh-eating mammal

clubfoot: a deformity that causes the foot to be misshapen and twisted out of position

dermal ridges: the equivalent of fingerprints, found only on humans and non-human primates

DNA: a complex molecule that carries genetic information

evidence: something that provides proof

evolution: the theory that various animals have changed over millions of years

extinct: no longer existing

Gigantopithecus: a presumed extinct gigantic ape, standing ten feet tall and weighing up to 1,200 pounds, that lived alongside humans for over a million years

hoax: an act intended to trick someone

hominin: a creature that is human or a human ancestor

Neanderthal: a hominin that lived from about 30,000 to 200,000 years ago

omnivore: an animal or person who eats meat and fish as well as plants and vegetables

primate: the classification of mammals that includes humans, apes, and monkeys

primitive: little evolved; belonging to an early state of development

quadruped: an animal that walks on four feet

sagittal crest: a bony ridge running lengthwise across the top of the skull like a Mohawk. The sagittal crest anchors muscles used for chewing and indicates the presence of strong jaw muscles.

scat: an animal dropping; poop

vegetarian: an animal or person who eats only vegetables, fruits, grains, nuts, and sometimes eggs or dairy products

vocalization: sound made with the voice

Bibliography & Further Reading

Books:

Burgan, Michael. *The Unexplained: Bigfoot*. Mankato, Minnesota: Capstone Press, 2005.

Cohen, Daniel. *The Encyclopedia of Monsters*. New York: Avon Books, 1991.

Coleman, Loren. *Mysterious America*. Winchester, Massachusetts: Faber & Faber, Inc., 1983.

Floyd, E. Randall. *Great American Mysteries*. Little Rock, Arkansas: House Publishers, 1990.

Gorman, Jacqueline Laks. *Bigfoot*. Milwaukee: Gareth Stevens Publishing, 2002.

Green, John. *Sasquatch: The Apes Among Us*. Seattle: Hancock House Publishers, 1978.

Herbst, Judith. *Monsters*. Minneapolis: Lerner Publications Company, 2005.

Hunter, Don, with René Dahinden. *Sasquatch: The Search for North America's Incredible Creature*. Buffalo, New York: Firefly Books, 1993.

Meldrum, Jeff. *Sasquatch: Legend Meets Science*. New York: Forge, 2006.

Morgan, Robert W. *Bigfoot Observer's Field Manual*. Enumclaw, Washington: Pine Winds Press, 2008.

Napier, J. *Bigfoot: The Yeti and Sasquatch in Myth and Reality*. New York: E.P. Dutton & Co., 1973.

Woog, Adam. *Mysterious Encounters: Bigfoot*. Farmington Hills, Michigan: Thomson Gale, 2006.

Videos:

Drachkovitch, Rasha, producer. *Ancient Mysteries: Bigfoot* (A&E Network). New York: New Video Group, 1994.

Lee, Julie, and Sheera von Puttkamer, producers. *Sasquatch Odyssey: The Hunt for Bigfoot*. Big Hairy Deal Films, Inc., 1999.

Websites:

Bigfoot Encounters (www.bigfootencounters.com)

Bigfoot Field Researchers Organization (www.bfro.net)

Bigfoot Lives (www.bigfoot-lives.com)

Bigfoot Museum (www.bigfootmuseum.com)

Cryptomundo (www.cryptomundo.com)

The Cryptozoologist (www.lorencoleman.com/cabinet_home.html)

Dean Harrison's Australian Yowie Research (www.yowiehunters.com)

Copyright © 2011 by Candlewick Press, Inc.

Illustrations by Mark Fearing.

Inspired by the theatrical motion picture *Judy Moody and the NOT Bummer Summer,* produced by Smokewood Entertainment Group, LLC

Judy Moody®. Judy Moody is a registered trademark of Candlewick Press, Inc.
Judy Moody font copyright © 2004 by Peter H. Reynolds

First edition 2011

Jacobs's Creature photograph page 31 copyright © by R. Jacobs.
All other photgraphs pages 30, 31 copyright © by Fortean Picture Library.

Library of Congress Cataloging-in-Publication Data is available.
Library of Congress Catalog Card Number 2010042546
ISBN 978-0-7636-5550-1

11 12 13 14 15 16 LBM 10 9 8 7 6 5 4 3 2 1

Printed in Melrose Park, IL, U.S.A.

This book was typeset in Officina.
The illustrations were digitally rendered.

Candlewick Press
99 Dover Street
Somerville, Massachusetts 02144

visit us at www.candlewick.com